FRIENDS
OF ACPL

HOLIDAY COLLECTION

A Christmas Star

Linda Oatman High

illustrated by Ronald Himler

Holiday House/New York

Text copyright © 1997 by Linda Oatman High
Illustrations copyright © 1997 by Ronald Himler
ALL RIGHTS RESERVED
Printed in the United States of America
FIRST EDITION

Library of Congress Cataloging-in-Publication Data
High, Linda Oatman.
A Christmas star / by Linda Oatman High: illustrated by Ron
Himler—[1st ed]
p.   cm.
Summary: A young girl looks forward to receiving mittens and
oranges and candy at church on a Christmas Eve during the
Depression, and when these special treats are stolen, her spirit sinks.
ISBN 0-8234-1301-2
[1. Christmas—Fiction.]   I. Himler, Ronald, ill.   II. Title.
PZ7.H543968Ch   1997   96-39131   CIP   AC
[E]—dc21

For Zach, with thanks to Erma Leinbach for answers about horses;
Nana, for magazines of the good old days;
and my parents for the magic of Santa Claus.

L.O.H.

A Christmas Eve moon gleams magical and full as we lead our horse, Star, into the yard where Granddaddy's old sleigh waits for Mama and Papa and me.

"Mitten tree, here I come," I say, shivering as we harness Star to reins jingling with sleigh bells. We drape the sleigh with angels of yarn and strings of popped corn, for we have no tree this Christmas.

"And now," says Papa, "let's decorate Star."

My eyes open wide as Papa ties on to Star a big velvet bow, a blanket soft and red, and antlers spiking high into the night.

"A Christmas Star," says Papa.

We climb into the sleigh and we're on our way to church for the Christmas Eve manger scene and the mitten tree, waiting with brand-new mittens for me.

"Where do all the mittens come from?" I ask, closing my eyes and remembering last year's tree, sprouting mittens in every color of the rainbow, hung high and low on its prickly green needles.

"From someone who cares," Mama says.

I blow warm air into my hands, wishing to be there, in the warm and cozy church, before the manger scene and near the mitten tree.

"Who brings the oranges and the candy?" I ask, taking the reins so that Papa can warm his hands.

"Saint Nicholas, of course," says Papa, shoving his hands deep into his pockets. "But he may not make it this Christmas, because of the Great Depression."

I sigh, guiding Star over roads piled high with snow, as the old sleigh creaks and squeaks.

"Where does the mitten tree come from?" I ask, thinking of how nobody I know has money to buy a tree for Christmas Eve.

"Pastor Sam's yard," says Mama. "He digs it up every year and plants it again when Christmas is finished."

"You have more questions," says Papa, putting his arm around me and drawing me close, "than Christmas has snow."

Below, in the valley shimmering with moonlit snow, glows our church, big and white and bright with lanterns and candles.

"I hope for mittens toasty as hot coals," I say, as Star and the sleigh glide down the hill and we make our way to the row of hitching posts in the back of the church. As Papa harnesses Star, I stomp my feet and think of the mittens I wish for—Christmas-red and snuggly-warm.

Walking toward the church, we pass a little barn, where Pastor Sam's animals wait for the manger scene. "The animals must love Christmas Eve," I say. "It's the only time they're allowed to come into the church."

"It's a magical time," Papa says, lifting me up high to peek inside the stalls.

I see the sow, and a lamb, and Bessie the cow, then stubborn old Beulah the mule, who always plays the part of the donkey. I smile, thinking of how Pastor Sam leads the animals one-by-one up the aisle, as the people clap and cheer.

Papa lowers me to the ground, and we all walk hand-in-hand toward the church for Christmas Eve: Mama and Papa and me. "I can't see the tree," I say as we walk. "It's always there, in that window." I point to a square of white light, empty and bright.

Papa pulls open the door and we push inside, feeling warmth burst upon our faces. My heart begins to pound, because people are angry and loud.

"Who would do such a thing?" asks a man.

Pastor Sam shakes his head. "Someone who doesn't care," he says.

I slide into a pew beside my best friend Emma.

"Someone took the mitten tree," she whispers. "And the candy, and the oranges."

My eyes fill with tears. No candy, no oranges, no tree. No mittens. No Christmas this year. Pastor Sam stands and everyone becomes quiet and still.

"They can steal our tree," says Pastor Sam. "They can steal our candy and our oranges and our mittens. But they can't steal Christmas."

The choir begins to hum and the piano keys sound sweet and loud as we all join in, singing the songs of Christmas. I sing, raising my voice high, but my heart falls to the floor.

"This is the worst Christmas ever," I whisper to Emma at the end of the singing.

She nods. "But at least we have the manger scene," she says, as Pastor Sam scatters straw upon the floor, and gathers together Wise Men and Shepherds and Angels and a Baby.

"Who will play Mary and Joseph this year?" Emma asks, and I shrug as Pastor Sam places the cradle upon the straw.

"Mary and Joseph," he calls and walks to the door.

I look around, seeing Mama and Papa rise to follow Pastor Sam outside. This is a surprise—Mama and Papa in the manger scene!

Emma and I go outside giggling. Mama and Papa are in the barn, and Mama perches on Beulah the mule, hiding a pillow inside her coat. Pastor Sam leads first the sow, then the lamb, then Bessie the cow, into the church. Papa stands by Mama's side, yanking upon Beulah's bridle and trying to guide the mule.

"Stubborn old Beulah," says Emma.

"She won't go," Papa calls to Pastor Sam, who is waiting at the door.

Pastor Sam hurries to Papa and tugs upon the straps.

"Beulah is the most bullheaded mule on earth," says Pastor Sam, as she balks and kicks and lowers her nose to the snow. "Maybe we could use a nice horse instead."

Beulah kicks again, twitches her ears, and brays at the sky, then lowers herself bucking to the snow, throwing Mama into the cold.

I look at Emma and she looks at me, and we both have the same idea.

"Star," I whisper, and we run together past the barn to the hitching posts. Through the dark, in the moonshine, I see Star's tail swishing from side to side, and hear her hooves pounding the ground.

"Star," I call, "you're going to be a star and play a part in the manger scene."

Suddenly, I stop in my tracks. "Emma," I whisper. "Do you see what I see?"

It's a man in a cap and coat and big black boots heaving something into our sleigh and then dashing away, disappearing like melted ice into the night.

"It was him," says Emma. "Saint Nicholas."

I look at Emma and she looks at me, and we both breathe fast and shaky.

"Santa Claus," I say, the words freezing in the air before my face. We go forward and I reach into the sleigh. My hands grasp a bag heavy and rough and I lift it, then drop it to the snow and pull it open.

"Candy," I whisper. "And oranges and toys." I reach into the bag and touch a pile soft and fuzzy.

"Mittens," I shout. "Lots and lots of mittens."

I pull the mittens onto my hands, reaching deep into the new wool. They fit just right, toasty warm as hot coals, and by the shine of the moon I see that they're red—Christmas-red, just as I wished.

"And there are more on Star's horns," Emma says, pointing. "More mittens."

I look up, then down, staring and staring at the mittens upon my hands. "It's magic," I tell her, as Star whinnies and tosses his head. I stand, handing the sack to Emma, and unharness Star from the post.

"Come on, Star," I say, leading him away. "It's time for you to shine."

We make our way to Mama and Papa, who gaze with wide eyes at Star's antlers and at the sack in Emma's hands.

"What's in the bag?" asks Papa, as I hand him Star's reins.

"Christmas," I say. "Saint Nicholas brought Christmas—candy and oranges and toys and mittens."

Papa looks at Mama and Mama looks at Papa, then they both look at Emma and me.

"Even the Great Depression couldn't keep Santa Claus away," I say, holding out my hands to show off my mittens.

"But where did they come from?" Papa asks, as Mama climbs upon Star's back.

"You have more questions," I say, putting my arm around Papa and drawing him close, "than Christmas has snow."

"It's a magical time," Papa says, shaking his head. Papa pats the white blaze on Star's face, then leads Star and Mama away toward the warm and cozy church.

Emma and I follow, holding the bag between us as Star moves through the door and plods slowly up the aisle, Papa in front. Mama sits tall and proud upon the red blanket, while the manger scene waits ahead, Wise Men and Shepherds and Angels and Baby all gazing in wonder as Star plods on and the people clap and cheer.

"Merry Christmas," I shout, reaching into the sack and grabbing handfuls of mittens. I toss them to children all through the church as Emma passes out oranges and candy and toys.

"They stole our tree but they didn't steal Christmas," says Pastor Sam as Mama and Papa and Star join the manger scene and the people become quiet and still.

"Who gave the gifts?" asks a man as Emma and I slide into a pew. "Someone who cares," I say and then smile and slip off my mittens, holding them close and warm next to my heart.